BEAR'S HICCUPS

BEAR'S HICCUPS

by Marion Dane Bauer
illustrated by
Diane Dawson Hearn

Holiday House/New York

For Katie,
who loves bears,
from Grandma,
who loves Katie.
M. D. B.

With thanks to Mary Cash.
D. D. H.

Text copyright © 1998 by Marion Dane Bauer
Illustrations copyright © 1998 by Diane Dawson Hearn
ALL RIGHTS RESERVED
Printed in the United States of America
FIRST EDITION
Library of Congress Cataloging-in-Publication Data
Bauer, Marion Dane.
Bear's Hiccups / by Marion Dane Bauer: illustrated by Diane
Dawson Hearn.—1st ed.
p.   cm.
Summary: On a hot summer day, while Bear and Frog are arguing
about who owns the cool, wet pond, Frog disappears and Bear develops
a sudden case of hiccups.
ISBN 0-8234-1339-X
[1. Bears—Fiction. 2. Frogs—Fiction. 3. Animals—Fiction.
4. Hiccups—Fiction.] I. Hearn, Diane Dawson, ill. II. Title.
PZ7.B3262Ho   1998   97-10881   CIP   AC
[E]—dc21

Contents

1. Looking for Trouble   6

2. Mine!   12

3. Grrrr!   18

4. Where Is Frog?   26

5. Cup-hic!   36

6. Frog, At Last   42

1.   Looking for Trouble

It was the hottest day
of the entire summer in the forest.
Every leaf on every tree
hung limp.
Flowers wilted.
Bees bumbled home for a nap.

The pond lay flat and still,

like a scarf dropped in the grass.

Otter was so hot he quit playing.

Frog was so hot he quit croaking.

Turtle was so hot she climbed

off her sunny rock.

She swam to the bottom

of the pond and buried herself

in the dark, cool mud.

But no one in all the forest
was hotter than Bear.
Her big, black nose was hot.
Her long, pink tongue was hot.
Her stubby tail was hot.
And everything in between
was hot as well.
Because she was hot,
Bear was also cross.
Because she was cross,
she was looking for trouble.
What she found was the pond,
as flat and still as a fallen scarf.

She poked her big, black nose
into the water.
The water was cool.
She dipped her long, pink tongue
into the water.
The water was wet.

Then she dropped her stubby tail
into the water.
And everything in between
her big, black nose
and her stubby tail
dropped in, too.

2. Mine!

Splash!

Minnows quivered away.

Big fish gasped.

Even Turtle stirred

in the dark, cool mud.

And Frog fell off his lily pad.

"This is a very small pond,"
Bear said.

"And I am a very large bear.
So the rest of you can go away.
This pond is mine. All mine."

Frog climbed onto his lily pad.

"What did you say?" he asked.

"What, what, what?"

Squirrel chattered.

"Mine," Bear said again.

Loudly.

Now, everyone in the forest
used that pond.
Everyone in the forest
needed that pond.
Everyone in the forest
loved that pond.
But no one used and needed
and loved it more than Frog.
Besides, he rather liked
the sound of the word, "Mine!"
But not when Bear said it.

So he bugged his eyes.

He puffed his chest.

And he sang the song he sang

every morning and evening

of the world.

"This is my pond, my pond,

my pond. Mine."

Then he added for good measure,

"Go away, Bear."

Turtle disappeared inside her shell.

The minnows held their breaths.

Even the lily pad trembled.

But Frog sat firm.

3. Grrrr!

Bear glared at Frog.

She growled.

Loudly.

"This pond is mine," she said.

"And everything in it is mine, too."

She came right up close to Frog.

"The water."

She came closer.

"That lily pad."

She came closer still.

"And you."

Bear poked her nose
into Frog's wide green face.

"Be careful, Frog!"
the minnows called.
"Watch, watch, watch out!"
Squirrel cried.
"Take care," Turtle pleaded.

"You are a very small frog.

And that is a very large bear."

But Frog did not like

being told what to do.

Not by a hot, cross Bear.

Not by his friends, either.

So he bugged his eyes.

He puffed his chest.

And he sang his song again.

And he sang it

right in Bear's face.

"This is my pond," he croaked.

"My pond, my pond,
my pond. Mine."
"MINE!" Bear roared back.
She opened her mouth so wide
that even the pond shuddered.

When she closed it again,

her teeth clacked together.

Loudly.

No one breathed.

No one moved.

No one spoke.

Until Turtle peeked

out of her shell,

swam to the surface of the pond,

and asked a quiet question.

"Where did Frog go?"

Bear's only reply was, "Hiccup!"

4. Where Is Frog?

"Where is Frog?"
  Turtle asked again.
"Yes, where is our friend Frog?"
  the minnows chorused.
"Hiccup!" Bear said once more.

Squirrel scolded
from a nearby tree.
"Stop, stop, stop, Bear!
You stop those hiccups now.
Tell us what you have done
with Frog."

"Hiccup, hiccup, hiccup!"
Bear said.
A big fish swam to the surface
of the pond.
"I will cure your hiccups,"
she said.
"But then you must tell us
where Frog is."
Bear growled and hiccuped
at the same time.
"She cannot answer,"
Bird declared.
"Just hold your breath,"
Fish ordered.
"Hold your breath
until you turn blue."

Bear glared at Fish.
But she held her breath
until her eyes turned red.
She held her breath
until her tongue turned purple.

She held her breath
until her claws turned blue.
Then she let it all out with a loud,
"Hiccup!"

Deer stepped out of the forest.

"When I have hiccups,"

she said softly,

"I drink water.

Lots and lots of water."

She touched her velvet lips

to the pond to show Bear the way.

Bear glared at Deer.

Still, Bear lapped water
with her tongue.
She sucked water
between her teeth.
She blew bubbles of water
out of her nose.
But when she lifted her head,
she could only say, "Hiccup!"
again.

Otter swam close to Bear.

"I know a cure," he offered.

"And it is fun, too."

"HICCUP!" Bear roared.

She glared at Otter.

"Just stand on your head,"
Otter said.

"Stand on your head
    as long as you can.
    Stand on your head
    until your hiccups stop."
    Then he dived beneath the water
    and hurried away.

5. Cup-hic!

Bear glared at the place
where Otter had been.
Then she stomped to a tree.
She put her head on the ground.
She put her tail in the air.
And everything in between
hung onto the tree.
Everyone watched.
Everyone waited.
And while they were waiting,
Bear said, "Cup-hic!"
in an upside-down way.
"Cup-hic. Cup!"

Now old turtles are known

to be patient creatures.

But this turtle was young.

And she was not patient yet.

She climbed out of the pond.

She marched to the tree.

She thrust her face

in Bear's upside-down face.

And she asked again

in her loudest voice,

"WHERE IS FROG?"

When she got no answer,
not even a hiccup,
she opened her toothless mouth
and bit Bear's nose.
Hard.

Everyone in the pond
was surprised.
Everyone in the forest
was surprised.

Though no one
in either pond or forest
was more surprised than Bear.
But when she tried to roar,
what came out instead was,
"AH CHOO!
AH CHOO! AH CHOO!
AH CHOO!"
And on the very last sneeze,
something popped out
of her mouth.

6.   Frog, At Last

There sat Frog.

Otter giggled.

Deer smiled and stepped silently
back into the forest.

The big fish chuckled.
Even Squirrel tittered
behind her bushy tail.
And the birds in the trees filled
the forest with bright laughter.
Turtle and Frog both grinned.

Bear glared at Turtle.

She glared at Frog.

She glared at everyone

and at no one at all.

She even glared at the pond.

Then grumbling to herself,

she climbed the tree,

walked out

onto the stoutest branch,

and lay down.

"This is a very small breeze,"

she said.

"And I am a very large bear.

So the rest of you can go away.

This breeze is mine. All mine."

No one said anything at all.

Except, of course, for Frog.

He climbed onto his lily pad.

He bugged his eyes.

He puffed his chest.

And he sang the song he sang
every morning and evening
of the world.

Only perhaps he sang it
a bit more quietly this time.
"This is my pond, my pond,
my pond. Mine."

And since it was the hottest day
of the entire summer
in the forest,
Turtle swam to the bottom
of their pond
and buried herself again
in the dark,
cool
mud.